# THERE'S A
# MOUSE
# IN THE
# HOUSE

Story & Illustrations by LUCIA TUTTLE

To order additional copies of this book, contact:
Xlibris Corporation
1-888-795-4274
www.Xlibris.com
Orders@Xlibris.com

*This book is dedicated to my dear granddaughters,*

*Miren & Madeleine.*

Once upon a time,

there lived a little mouse,

and his home was in the kitchen

of a big, old house.

"I'm a happy little mouse," said he, said he.

"Of all the mousies in the world,
I'd rather be me!"

And he jumped,

and he laughed,

and he squeaked with glee,

"I'm a happy little mouse,
and I'm happy to be me!"

He would sleep all day,

then he'd play all night,

as he ran to the kitchen for a tasty bite.

To the table, to the breadbox, to the cupboard
near the door, no matter how much food
he ate, there'd always be lots more.

And he jumped, and he laughed,

and he squeaked with glee,

"I'm a happy little mouse,
and I'm happy to be me!"

But then one night, as he nibbled on some cheese,
he sprinkled it with pepper,
and the pepper made him sneeze!

"ACHOO!" said he, then he began to worry.
Suppose someone had heard him,
he said, "I'd better scurry."

So he scurried in a hurry, and there was
an awful clutter,

as he tripped on a crumb and left his
footprint in the butter!

Then he ran to his bed,
where he covered up his head
-- all except one ear --
and he heard a voice that said:

"ME THINKS THERE'S A MOUSE IN THE HOUSE."

Mousie heard this voice,
and his heart was filled with fear,
for those were the words
he'd been dreading to hear:

"ME THINKS THERE'S A MOUSE IN THE HOUSE."

"And I'm that mouse," said he, said he. "Oh, dear, they know I'm here. I used to laugh and squeak with glee, but now I'm filled with fear."

The poor little mouse, afraid in his own house, and he wiped away a tear.

But late that night,

when the whole house slept,

he peeked out carefully,

then from his hole he crept.

No traps could he see as he ventured on his way,

so he hummed a little tune, then began

to laugh and say:

"HO HO, HEE HEE, I'm so happy to be me! Although

they know I'm in the house, no one will bother a

poor little mouse."

And he jumped, and he laughed,

and he squeaked with glee,

"I'm a happy little mouse,
and I'm happy to be me!"

Then he jumped to the cracker box,
and lifted up the lid.

He reached inside to take one,
and just as he did...

ZZZZZ-INGO!

And someone said, "AH HA!"

Then the mouse was in the clutches
of a big and furry paw!

"This house is MY house," said a big, old cat.
"And now I've got you, Mousie.
How do you like that?"

The little mouse was frightened, he could
barely speak, but this is what he answered
in a tiny little squeak:

"I'm a homely
little mouse,"
said he,
said he.

"What would such a pretty cat want with me?"

"Do you really think I'm pretty?"
said the big,
old cat.

"Golly, it's been
many years
since
someone
told me
that."

"Yes, I really think you're pretty,"
said the frightened little mouse.

"Why can't we be friends
and live together in this house?"

"Friends?" said the cat. "You'd be friends with me? I've never ever had a friend,

I'm not too nice, you see."

Mousie said, "I think you're nice,
as well as being pretty.

You can call me 'Mousie,'
and I'll call you 'Miss Kitty.'"

"Mousie," said the cat, with a tear in her eye. "It's very nice to have a friend, I think I'm going to cry!"

And she sobbed, "BOO HOO," until her nose was turning blue.

"I'm so happy to have found a friend, I don't know what to do!"

"It's easy, dear Miss Kitty, now
hear this one small clue:

If you want someone to like you,
you've got to like him, too."

And from that night on,
Miss Kitty and the Mouse,
they lived and played
together
in the
big, old house.

"It's easy to be friendly, if you're good
and kind and true."

Take this advice from Mousie,
He's talking right to YOU!

And he jumped, and he laughed,

and he squeaked with glee,

"I'm a happy little mouse,
and I'm happy to be me!"

"And I'm happy, too," said Miss Kitty.